Jack put the rainforest book in his rucksack. Then he stepped onto the rope ladd'

He started to climb down. Annie followed with Peanut in her pocket.

Jack pushed through the leaves.

He came to the understory below the canopy.

He looked down at the forest floor. It was very far away.

"Oh, wow," whispered Jack.

This world was completely different from the one above the treetops.

Now that they were out of the sun, it was cooler. It was also damp and very quiet.

Jack shivered. It was the spookiest place he had ever seen.

*Read all the adventures of **Jack** and **Annie**!*

Coming soon . . .

Magic Tree House™

ADVENTURE on the AMAZON

MARY POPE OSBORNE

Illustrated by Philippe Masson

RED FOX

ADVENTURE ON THE AMAZON
A RED FOX BOOK 978 1 862 30567 0

First published in Great Britain by Red Fox,
an imprint of Random House Children's Books
A Random House Group Company

Published in the US by Random House Children's Books,
a division of Random House Inc, 1995

Red Fox edition published 2008

1 3 5 7 9 10 8 6 4 2

The Random House Group Limited supports The Forest Stewardship
Council® (FSC®), the leading international forest certification organisation.
All our titles that are printed on Greenpeace approved FSC® certified paper
carry the FSC® logo. Our paper procurement policy can be found at
www.randomhouse.co.uk/environment

MIX
Paper from
responsible sources
FSC® C016897

Set in Bembo Schoolbook

Red Fox Books are published by Random House Children's Books,
61–63 Uxbridge Road, London W5 5SA

www.kidsatrandomhouse.co.uk

Addresses for companies within The Random House Group Limited can be found at:
www.randomhouse.co.uk/offices.htm

THE RANDOM HOUSE GROUP Limited Reg. No. 954009

A CIP catalogue record for this book is available from the British Library.

Printed in the UK by CPI Bookmarque, Croydon, CR0 4TD

For Piers Pope Boyce

Contents

Prologue

One summer day in Frog Valley, a mysterious tree house appeared in the woods.

Eight-year-old Jack and his seven-year-old sister, Annie, climbed into the tree house. They found that it was filled with books.

Jack and Annie soon discovered that the tree house was magic. It could take them to the places in the books. All they had to do was point to a picture and wish to be there.

Jack and Annie visited the time of dinosaurs, knights, pyramids, pirates and ninjas. Along the way, they discovered that the tree house belonged to Morgan le Fay. Morgan is a magical librarian from the time of King Arthur. She travels through time and space, gathering books.

In their last adventure, *Night of the Ninjas*, Jack and Annie learned that Morgan was under a spell. To free her, Jack and Annie have to find four special things.

In ancient Japan, they found the first thing: a moonstone.

Now Jack and Annie are about to set out in search of the second thing . . . in *Adventure on the Amazon*.

1

Where's Peanut?

"Hurry, Jack!" shouted Annie.

She ran into the Frog Valley woods.

Jack followed her.

"It's still here!" Annie called.

Jack caught up with her. She was standing beside a tall oak tree.

Jack looked up. The magic tree house was shining in the afternoon sunlight.

"We're coming, Peanut!" Annie called.

She grabbed the rope ladder and started to climb up.

Jack followed. They climbed and

climbed. Finally they climbed into the tree house.

"Peanut?" said Annie.

Jack took off his rucksack. He looked around.

Sunlight slanted across a stack of books – books about ninjas, pirates, mummies, knights and dinosaurs.

The letter M shimmered on the wooden floor. M for Morgan le Fay.

"I don't think Peanut's here," said Jack.

"I wonder where she is," said Annie.

"How do you know Peanut's a *she*?" asked Jack.

"I just know it," said Annie.

Squeak!

Annie laughed. "Look, Jack!"

A small pink sock was moving across the floor. Yesterday Annie had turned her sock into a bed for Peanut.

Annie picked up the tiny lump.

Squeak.

A brown-and-white mouse peeped out of the sock. She looked from Annie to Jack with her big eyes.

Jack laughed. "Hi, Peanut," he said.

"Will you help us again today?" asked Annie.

In ancient Japan, Peanut had helped them when they got lost.

"We have to find three more things for Morgan," said Annie.

Jack pushed his glasses into place. "First we have to find a clue that tells us where to begin," he said.

"Guess what," said Annie.

"What?" said Jack.

"We don't have to look very far." She pointed at a corner of the tree house.

In the shadows was an open book.

2

Creepy-Crawlies

"Wow," said Jack, picking up the book. "The ninja book was open yesterday. Now this one. Who opened them?"

He closed the book and looked at the cover.

It showed a picture of a green forest. The trees were very tall and close together.

On the cover were the words *The Rainforest*.

"Oh, wow," said Jack.

"Oh, no," said Annie.

"What's wrong?" said Jack.

"I learned about the rainforest at school," said Annie. "It's filled with creepy-crawlies."

"I know," said Jack. "Half of them have never even been named."

"It's creepy," said Annie.

"It's great," said Jack. He wanted to take lots of notes in the rainforest. Maybe he could even name some unknown insects.

"Great? Yuck," said Annie. She shivered.

"I don't understand," said Jack. "You weren't afraid of dinosaurs."

"So?"

"You weren't afraid of the castle guards or the mummy's ghost."

"So?"

"You weren't afraid of pirates or ninjas."

"So?"

"You're not afraid of *really* scary things. But you're afraid of little insects. That doesn't make sense."

"*So?*"

Jack sighed. "Listen," he said. "We have to go there. To help Morgan. That's why the book was left open."

"I know that," said Annie, frowning.

"Plus, the rainforests are being cut down," said Jack. "Don't you want to see one before it's too late?"

Annie took a deep breath and slowly nodded.

"OK, then, let's go," said Jack.

He opened the book again. He pointed to a picture that showed blue sky, green leaves and bright flowers.

"I wish we could go there," he said.

The wind began to blow.

Squeak.

"Stay here, Peanut," said Annie as she put the mouse in her pocket.

The wind picked up. The tree house started to spin.

Jack squeezed his eyes shut.

The wind was whistling now. The tree house was spinning faster and faster.

Then everything was still.

Absolutely still.

Wild sounds broke the silence.

Screeeeeech!

Buzzzzzzz!

Chirp! Chirp!

11

3
Oh, No!

Jack opened his eyes.

The air was hot and steamy.

"It looks like we've landed in some bushes," said Annie.

She was peeping out of the tree-house window. Peanut was peeping out of Annie's pocket.

Jack peeped out of the tree house too.

They had landed in a sea of shiny green leaves. Outside there were flowers, bright butterflies and birds. Just like the book.

"That's strange," said Jack. "I wonder why we didn't land in a tree. The way we always do."

"I don't know," said Annie. "But let's hurry and find the thing for Morgan. Then we can get back home before we meet any big insects."

"Wait. This seems weird," said Jack. "I

13

don't understand why we landed in some bushes. I'd better read about this."

"Oh, come on," said Annie. "We don't even need the ladder. We can just climb out of the window."

Annie put Peanut in her pocket. She stuck one leg out of the window.

"Wait!" Jack grabbed Annie's other leg. He read:

The rainforest is in three layers. Thick treetops, often over 50 metres high, make up the top layer. This is called the forest canopy. Below the canopy is the understorey, then the forest floor.

"Get back in here!" cried Jack. "We're probably more than fifty metres above the ground! In the forest canopy!"

"Oh, no!" said Annie. She slipped

back into the tree house.

"We *have* to use the ladder," said Jack. He got down on his hands and knees. He moved leaves away from the hole in the floor. He looked down.

The ladder seemed to fall between the branches of a giant tree. But Jack couldn't see beyond that.

"I can't tell what's down there," he said. "Be careful."

Jack put the rainforest book in his rucksack. Then he stepped onto the rope ladder.

He started to climb down. Annie followed with Peanut in her pocket.

Jack pushed through the leaves.

He came to the understorey below the canopy.

He looked down at the forest floor. It was very far away.

"Oh, wow," whispered Jack.

This world was completely different from the one above the treetops.

Now that they were out of the sun, it was cooler. It was also damp and very quiet.

Jack shivered. It was the spookiest place he had ever seen.

4

Millions of Them!

Jack didn't move. He kept staring down at the forest floor.

"What's wrong?" Annie called from above.

Jack didn't answer.

"You don't see any giant spiders, do you?" Annie said.

"Well . . . no." Jack took a deep breath.

We have to keep going, he thought. We have to find the special thing for Morgan.

Jack and Annie climbed down
through the understorey. Finally
they stepped onto the forest floor.
Only a few rays of light slanted
through the gloom.

The trees were very, very tall
and very wide. Creepers and moss
were hanging everywhere. The
ground was covered with dead
leaves.

"Before we do anything, I'd better check the book," said Jack.

He pulled out the rainforest book. He found a picture of the dark world under the treetops. He read:

In the rainforest, many living creatures blend in with their surroundings. This is called camouflage.

"Oh, wow," said Jack. He closed the book and looked around. "There're *lots* of creatures down here. We just can't see them."

"Really?" whispered Annie.

She and Jack peered around at the quiet forest. Jack felt unseen eyes watching them.

"Let's hurry and find the special thing," whispered Annie.

"How will we know when we find it?" Jack said.

"I think we'll just know," said Annie. She headed off through the gloom.

Jack followed. They crept between the huge trees and past hanging creepers.

Annie stopped. "Wait – what's that?"

"What's what?"

"Listen – that weird sound."

Jack listened. He heard a crackling sound.

It sounded like a person walking over leaves.

Jack looked around. He didn't see anyone.

But the sound got louder.

Was it an animal? A giant insect? One that had never been named?

Just then the silent forest came alive.

Birds flew off into the air. Frogs hopped over the leaves. Lizards ran up the tree trunks.

The weird noise grew louder and louder.

"Maybe the book explains it," said Jack. He opened the book. He found a picture of different animals running together. He read:

When animals hear a crackling sound, they flee in panic. The sound means that 30 million flesh-eating army ants are marching through the dead leaves.

"It's army ants!" cried Jack. "Millions of them!"

"Where?" cried Annie.

Jack and Annie looked around wildly.

"There!"
Annie pointed.
Army ants –
millions and
millions of
them – were
marching
over the leaves!
"Run to
the tree house!"
cried Annie.

"Where is it?" said Jack, whirling round. All the trees looked the same. Where was the rope ladder?

"Just run!" cried Annie.

Jack and Annie set off.

They ran over the dead leaves.

They ran between wide tree trunks.

They ran past the hanging creepers and moss.

24

They climbed over thick roots.

Jack saw a clearing ahead. It was filled with sunlight.

"That way!" he cried.

Jack and Annie hurried towards the light. They pushed their way through the bushes.

They burst out onto the bank of a river.

They stared at the slow-moving brown water.

"Do you think the ants will come this way?" Annie said, panting.

"I don't know," said Jack. "But if we wade a couple of metres into the river, we'll be safe. The ants won't go into the water. Come on."

"Look!" said Annie.

She pointed to a big log rocking at the edge of the river. The inside of the log was dug out.

"It looks like a canoe," said Jack. He listened to the crackling sound in the distance. "Let's get in it. Quick!"

Jack shoved the book into his rucksack. Then he and Annie carefully climbed into the dug-out log.

Annie leaned out of it. She pushed away from the bank with her hands.

"Wait!" said Jack. "We don't have any paddles!"

"Oops," said Annie.

The canoe started moving slowly down the muddy river.

5

Pretty Fish

Squeak.

Annie patted the little mouse in her pocket.

"It's OK, Peanut. The ants can't get us in the river. We're safe," she said.

"Maybe safe from the ants," said Jack. "But where is this canoe going?"

Jack and Annie stared at the river. Branches spread over the water. Creepers and moss hung down from them.

"We'd better look this up," said Jack. He pulled the rainforest book out of

his rucksack and
flipped through it.

Soon he found a
picture of a river. He
read:

*The Amazon River
stretches over 4000 miles
from the mountains of Peru,
across Brazil, to the Atlantic
Ocean. The river basin
contains over half of the
rainforests in the world.*

Jack looked at Annie. "We're on the Amazon River," he said. "It's more than four thousand miles long!"

"Wow," Annie whispered. She looked at the river. She trailed her hand through the water.

"I have to make some notes," Jack said. He pulled his notebook out of his bag. He wrote:

The Amazon rainforest is

"Jack, look at those pretty fish with the teeth," said Annie.

"What?" Jack glanced up from his writing.

Annie was pointing at some blue fish

swimming near the boat. The fish had red bellies and razor-sharp teeth.

"Watch it!" cried Jack. "Those aren't pretty fish. They're piranhas! They'll eat anything! Even people!"

"Oh, no," whispered Annie.

"We better get back to the shore," said Jack, putting the books in his rucksack.

"How?" said Annie. "We can't go in the water now. And we don't have any paddles."

Jack tried to stay calm. "We need a plan," he said.

He stared at the river. The canoe would soon float under some creepers.

"I'll grab a creeper," said Jack. "And pull us to shore."

"Good idea," said Annie.

As they glided under the branches, Jack stood up.

The canoe rocked. He nearly fell out.

"Balance the canoe," said Jack.

Annie leaned to one side. Jack reached – and missed!

The canoe floated under more branches.

Jack reached for another thick creeper.

He grabbed it!

It was cold and scaly. It wiggled and jerked!

"*Ahhh!*" Jack screamed and fell back into the canoe.

The creeper was alive!

It was a long green snake!

The snake fell from the tree. It splashed into the water and swam away.

Jack and Annie stared in horror at each other.

"What now?" said Annie, making a face.

"Well . . ." Jack looked at the river. There were no creepers up ahead. But there was a big branch floating on the water.

"Grab that branch near you," said Jack. "Maybe we can use it as a paddle."

The canoe floated closer to the branch. Annie reached for it.

Suddenly the branch rose into the air!

It was a *crocodile*!

"Help!" screamed Annie, and she fell back into the canoe.

The crocodile opened and closed its huge, long jaws. Then it moved past the canoe and swam up the river.

"Oh, no," whispered Jack.

A screeching sound split the air.

Jack and Annie jumped.

"Help!" said Jack.

He expected to see another terrible creature.

But all he saw was a small brown monkey, hanging by its tail from a tree.

6

Monkey Trouble

Squeak! Squeak! Peanut poked her head out of Annie's pocket. She seemed to be yelling at the monkey.

"Don't worry, Peanut," said Annie. "He's just a little monkey. He won't hurt us."

But suddenly the monkey grabbed a big red fruit hanging from the tree. He hurled it at the canoe.

"Watch it!" shouted Jack.

The fruit fell into the water with a splash.

The monkey screeched even louder.

He grabbed another fruit.

"Don't throw things at us!" shouted Annie.

But the monkey hurled the red fruit right at them.

Jack and Annie ducked again. And the fruit splashed into the water.

"Stop that!" Annie shouted.

But the monkey only waved his arms and screeched again.

"Oh, no," said Jack. "I don't believe this."

The monkey grabbed a third fruit and threw it at Jack and Annie. It landed inside the canoe with a thump.

Annie grabbed the fruit. She stood up and threw it back at the monkey.

She missed. The canoe rocked. Annie almost fell out.

The monkey screeched even louder.

"Go away!" Annie shouted. "You're the nastiest thing in the world!"

The monkey stopped screeching.

He looked at Annie. Then he swung away. Into the forest.

"I think I hurt his feelings," said Annie.

"Who cares?" said Jack. "He shouldn't throw things."

"Uh-oh," said Annie. "It's raining now."

"What?" Jack looked up. A raindrop hit him in the eye.

"Oh, no. I don't believe this," he said.

"What'd you expect?" said Annie. "It *is* the rainforest."

A gust of wind blew the canoe.

Thunder rolled in the sky.

"A river's a bad place to be in a storm," said Jack. "We have to get back to the shore. Right now."

"But how?" said Annie. "We can't wade or swim. The piranhas, the snake and the crocodile will get us."

Screeching split the air again.

"Oh, no," said Jack. The mischievous monkey was back.

This time, the monkey was pointing a long stick at the canoe.

Jack crouched down. Was the monkey going to hurl the stick at them? Like a spear?

Annie jumped up and faced the monkey.

"Watch it! He's crazy," said Jack.

But the monkey just stared at Annie. And Annie just stared back at him.

After a long moment, the monkey seemed to smile.

Annie smiled back.

"What's going on?" said Jack.

"He wants to help us," Annie said.

"Help us how?" said Jack.

The monkey held out the long stick. Annie grabbed the other end.

The monkey pulled on the stick. The canoe started floating towards him.

The monkey pulled the canoe all the way to the bank of the river.

7

Freeze!

Jack and Annie jumped out of the canoe.

The rain was starting to fall harder.

The monkey set off. He swung from tree to tree, heading up the riverbank.

He screeched and beckoned to Jack and Annie.

"He wants us to follow him!" said Annie.

"No! We have to find the special thing. Then go home!" said Jack.

"He wants to help us!" said Annie. She set off after the monkey.

The two of them vanished into the rainforest.

"Annie!"

Thunder shook the sky.

Jack dashed after Annie and the monkey. Into the dark forest.

The forest seemed surprisingly dry.

Jack looked up. It was still raining. But the treetops acted like a huge umbrella.

"Annie?" he called.

"Jack! Jack!" cried Annie.

"Where are you?"

"Here!"

Jack hurried in the direction of Annie's voice.

Soon he found the monkey. He was screeching and swinging from a tree.

Annie was kneeling on the forest floor. She was playing with an animal that looked like a giant kitten.

"What's that?" Jack said.

"I don't know, but I love it!" said Annie.

She stroked the animal's paws. It had gold fur and black spots.

"I'd better find out what it is," said Jack.

He pulled out the rainforest book and flipped through it.

"Oh, it's so sweet," said Annie.

Jack found a picture of an animal with gold fur and black spots. He read:

The jaguar is the biggest predator in the western hemisphere.

"Forget sweet," Jack said. "That must be a baby jaguar. It's going to grow up and be the biggest predator in—"

"What's a predator?" asked Annie.

GRRR! There was a terrible growl.

Jack whirled round.

The mother jaguar was coming out from behind a tree. She was creeping over the dead leaves – *right towards Annie.*

"Freeze!" whispered Jack.

Annie froze. But the jaguar
kept moving slowly towards
her.

"Help!" said Jack weakly.
Suddenly the monkey
swooped down from his tree.
He grabbed the jaguar's tail!
The cat roared and spun
round.

Annie jumped up.

The monkey pulled the jaguar's tail
again. Then he let go and set off.

The jaguar sprang after him.

"Run, Annie!" cried Jack.

Jack and Annie set off
through the rainforest. They
ran for their lives!

8

Vampire Bats?

"Wait," said Jack, panting. "I think we've got away."

Jack and Annie stopped running and caught their breath.

"Where are we?" said Jack.

"Where's the monkey?" said Annie, looking back at the forest. "Do you think the jaguar caught him?"

"No, monkeys are fast," said Jack.

Of course, jaguars are fast too, he thought. But he didn't want to tell Annie that.

"I hope he's OK," said Annie.

Squeak. Peanut peeped out of Annie's pocket.

"Peanut! I almost forgot about you!" said Annie. "Are you OK?"

The mouse just stared at Annie with her big eyes.

"She looks scared," said Jack. "Poor Peanut."

"Poor monkey," said Annie. She looked around at the forest.

"We'd better check the book," Jack said.

He pulled out the book. He turned the pages, searching for help.

He stopped at a picture of a scary creature.

"Oh, no. What's this?" he said.

Jack read the writing below the picture. It said:

Vampire bats live in the Amazon rainforest. At night, they quietly bite their victims and suck their blood.

"Vampire bats?" said Jack. He felt faint.

"Vampire bats?" said Annie.

Jack nodded. "After dark."

Annie and Jack looked around. The rainforest seemed to be getting even darker.

"Oh, no," said Annie. She looked at Jack. "Maybe we should go home."

Jack nodded. For once he agreed with her.

"But what about our mission?" said Annie. "What about Morgan?"

"We'll come back," said Jack. "We'll have to be prepared."

"So we'll come back tomorrow?" Annie asked.

"Right. Now which way is the tree house?" said Jack.

"This way," said Annie, pointing.

"That way," said Jack, pointing in the opposite direction.

They looked at each other. "We're lost," they said together.

Squeak.

"Don't worry, Peanut." Annie started to pat the mouse again. But then she stopped.

Squeak. Squeak. Squeak.

"Jack, I think Peanut wants to help us," said Annie.

"How?"

"The way she helped us in the time of the ninjas."

Annie placed the mouse on the leafy forest floor. "Take us to the tree house, Peanut."

The mouse set off.

"Where's she gone?" said Annie. "I can't see her!"

"There!" said Jack. He pointed to leaves rustling on the ground.

A streak of white passed over the leaves.

"Yes, there!" said Annie.

Jack and Annie followed the moving leaves. The streak of white appeared. And disappeared.

Suddenly Jack stopped.

The forest floor was still. There was no sign of Peanut.

"Where is she?" asked Jack.

He kept staring at the ground.

"Jack!"

Jack glanced round. Annie was standing on the other side of a nearby tree. She was pointing up.

Jack looked up.

The tree house.

"Oh, phew," Jack said softly.

"She's saved us again," said Annie. "She's running up the ladder. All by herself. Look."

She pointed at the rope ladder.

Peanut was climbing up one of the ropes.

"Let's go," Jack said.

Annie started up the ladder. Then Jack.

They followed Peanut all the way up to the canopy of the rainforest.

9
The Thing

Jack and Annie climbed into the tree house.

Peanut was sitting on a stack of books.

Annie patted Peanut's little head. "Thanks," she said softly.

"I have to write some notes about the rainforest," said Jack. "You find the Frog Valley book."

Annie began searching for the book – the one that always took them home.

Jack pulled out his notebook.

He had wanted to take lots of notes

59

here. But all he'd written so far was:

The Amazon rainforest is

"It's not here!" said Annie.

"What?" Jack looked up. He glanced around the tree house.

Annie was right. The Frog Valley book was nowhere in sight.

"Was it here before we left the woods?" said Jack.

"I can't remember," said Annie.

"Oh, no," said Jack. "Now we can't get back to Frog Valley."

"That means we'll

be here when the vampire bats come out," said Annie.

Something came flying through the tree-house window.

"Ahhh!" Jack and Annie hid their heads.

Thud.

Something hit the floor. A red fruit.

Jack looked up. The monkey was sitting in the window. His head was cocked to one side. He seemed to be grinning at them.

"You're safe!" said Annie.

"Thanks for saving us," said Jack.

The monkey just grinned.

"I have just one question," said Annie. She pointed at the fruit. "Why do you keep throwing those at us?"

The monkey grabbed the fruit.

"No! Don't throw it!" said Jack. He ducked.

But the monkey didn't throw the fruit.

He held it out to Annie. He moved his lips as if he were trying to say something.

Annie stared into the monkey's eyes. He moved his lips again. "Wow," Annie said softly. "I understand now."

"Understand what?" said Jack.

Annie took the fruit from the monkey. "This is it," she said. "The *thing* we need."

"What thing?" said Jack.

"One of the special things we're supposed to find for Morgan," Annie said. "To free her from the spell."

"Are you sure?" said Jack.

Before Annie could answer, Jack saw the Frog Valley book. "Look! Our book!" he said, pointing.

"We found the thing. And now we can see the book," said Annie. "That's the way it works, remember?"

Jack nodded. Now he remembered. The ninja master said they wouldn't be able to find the Frog Valley book until they had found what they were looking for.

The monkey screeched with laughter.

Jack and Annie looked at him. He was clapping his hands together.

Annie laughed with him. "How did

you know to give this to us?" she said.
"Who told you to do that?"

The monkey just waved at Jack and
Annie. Then he turned and swung away
out of the tree house.

"Wait!" said Jack, looking out of the
window.

Too late.

The monkey was gone. He had
vanished below the treetops.

"Goodbye!" called Annie.

A happy screech came from the
mysterious world below.

Jack sighed. He picked up his notebook
again. He looked at his writing:

The Amazon rain forest
is

He had to write *something* before they

left. He quickly added

amazing

Jack put away his notebook. Annie picked up the Frog Valley book.

"Now it's really time to leave," she said.

She turned to the picture of the woods. "I wish we could go there," she said, pointing at the picture.

The wind started to blow.

The leaves began to tremble.

The tree house began to spin.

It spun faster and faster.

Then everything was still.

Absolutely still.

10

Halfway There

Squeak.

Jack opened his eyes. Peanut was on the tree-house windowsill.

"We're home," said Annie.

Jack breathed a sigh of relief.

Annie held the fruit up to the afternoon light.

"What exactly *is* this?" she asked.

"Maybe it's in the book," Jack answered.

He pulled out the rainforest book. He flipped through the pages. He came to a picture of the red fruit.

"Here it is!" he said. He read out loud: "*The mango has a sweet taste like that of a peach.*"

"Mango? Hmmm," said Annie. She brought the fruit close to her lips.

"Hey!" said Jack, grabbing the mango from her. "We have to put it with the moonstone."

Jack placed the mango on the M carved into the floor. Next to the clear moonstone.

"Moonstone . . . mango," whispered Annie. It sounded like a spell.

"We're halfway there," said Jack. "Two more to go."

"Then we can free you, Morgan!" Annie called, as if Morgan were nearby.

"How do you know she can hear you?" said Jack.

"I can just feel it," Annie said.

"Hmmm," said Jack. He needed more proof than that.

Squeak. Peanut was looking at Jack and Annie.

"We have to leave you now," Jack said to the mouse.

Squeak.

"Can't we take her with us?" said Annie.

"No," said Jack. "Mum won't let us keep a mouse in the house. She doesn't like mice, remember?"

"How could anyone not like a mouse?" said Annie.

Jack smiled. "How could anyone not like a spider?" he said.

"That's different." Annie patted

Peanut's head. "Bye," she said. "Wait for us here. We'll be back tomorrow."

Jack patted the mouse too. "Bye, Peanut. Thanks for your help," he said.

Squeak.

Jack put the rainforest book on top of the book about ninjas.

Then he pulled on his rucksack. And he and Annie left the tree house.

They climbed down the rope ladder. They stepped onto the ground.

They started walking through the Frog Valley woods.

Leaf shadows danced in the light.

A bird called out.

These woods are very different from the rainforest, Jack thought.

"There're no jaguars or army ants here," he said. "No little monkeys."

"You know, that monkey was never

being nasty," said Annie. "He was just trying to give us the mango."

"I know. Actually, nothing was being nasty," said Jack. "The army ants were just marching. That's what army ants do."

"The piranhas were just being piranhas," said Annie.

"The snake was just being a snake," said Jack.

"The crocodile was just being a crocodile," said Annie.

"The jaguar was just taking care of her baby," said Jack.

Annie shuddered. "I still don't love insects," she said.

"You don't have to *love* them," said Jack. "Just leave them alone. And they won't bother you."

In fact, that's true about the whole rainforest, Jack thought. Everyone should just leave it all alone.

"Who cares if the insects don't have names?" he said softly. "*They* know who they are."

Jack and Annie stepped out of the Frog Valley woods.

They started walking up their street. It was lit with a golden light.

"Race you!" said Annie.

They set off running.

They ran across their garden.

They raced up their steps.

"Safe!" they shouted together as they reached their front door.